What Is in the Box?

big & SMALL

Original Korean text © Eom Mi-rang
Illustrations copyright © Choi Hye-in
Original Korean edition © Sigongsa Co., Ltd. 2009

This English edition published by Big & Small in 2014
by arrangement with Sigongsa Co., Ltd.
English text edited by Joy Cowley
English edition © Big & Small 2014

ISBN: 978-1-921790-80-5

Printed in Korea

What Is in the Box?

Written by Eom Mi-rang Illustrated by Choi Hye-in
Edited by Joy Cowley

What will Teddy do today?

Teddy tips up the box
and things fall out.
Look at the colours!

Here is a **red** fire engine.
What else is **red**?

Here are some **orange** carrots.
What else is **orange**?

Here are some **yellow** bubbles.
What else is **yellow**?

Here are some **green** paper aeroplanes.
What else is **green**?

The submarine is **blue**.
What else is **blue**?

The paintbrush has **indigo** paint.
Here is an **indigo** bird.
What else is **indigo**?

Teddy looks in the box.
Nothing left!

Mouse comes with a **violet** ball.
Teddy and Mouse play
with the **violet** ball.

Red, orange, yellow,
green, blue, indigo
and violet.

These are the colours
of the rainbow!